LITTLE GRUNT
and the
BIG EGG

A PREHISTORIC FAIRY TALE

Tomie dePaola

G. P. Putnam's Sons

For Barbara,
who has dinosaurs on her car dashboard.

G. P. PUTNAM'S SONS

A division of Penguin Young Readers Group.

Published by The Penguin Group.

Penguin Group (USA) Inc., 375 Hudson Street, New York, NY 10014, U.S.A.

Penguin Group (Canada), 90 Eglinton Avenue East, Suite 700, Toronto, Ontario, Canada M4P 2Y3

(a division of Pearson Penguin Canada Inc.).

Penguin Books Ltd, 80 Strand, London WC2R 0RL, England.

Penguin Ireland, 25 St. Stephen's Green, Dublin 2, Ireland (a division of Penguin Books Ltd.).

Penguin Group (Australia), 250 Camberwell Road, Camberwell, Victoria 3124, Australia

(a division of Pearson Australia Group Pty Ltd).

Penguin Books India Pvt Ltd, 11 Community Centre, Panchsheel Park, New Delhi - 110 017, India.

Penguin Group (NZ), Cnr Airborne and Rosedale Roads, Albany, Auckland 1310, New Zealand

(a division of Pearson New Zealand Ltd).

Penguin Books (South Africa) (Pty) Ltd, 24 Sturdee Avenue, Rosebank, Johannesburg 2196, South Africa.

Penguin Books Ltd, Registered Offices: 80 Strand, London WC2R 0RL, England.

Manufactured in China by South China Printing Co. Ltd.

Design by Katrina Damkoehler. Text set in Advert.

Library of Congress Cataloging-in-Publication Data

De Paola, Tomie. Little Grunt and the big egg : a prehistoric fairy tale / Tomie dePaola.   p. cm.

Summary: When a dinosaur hatches from the egg that Little Grunt brought home for dinner,

Mama and Papa Grunt let him keep it as a pet until it grows too big for their cave.

[1. Dinosaurs—Fiction. 2. Pets—Fiction. 3. Cave dwellers—Fiction.] I. Title.

PZ7.D439Li 2006   [E]—dc22   2005023965

ISBN 0-399-24529-4

1 3 5 7 9 10 8 6 4 2

First Impression

Once upon a time, in a big cave, past the volcano on the left, lived the Grunt Tribe. There was Unca Grunt, Ant Grunt, Granny Grunt, Mama Grunt, and Papa Grunt. Their leader was Chief Rockhead Grunt. The smallest Grunt of all was Little Grunt.

"Little Grunt," said Mama Grunt,
"the Ugga-Wugga Tribe is coming for
Sunday brunch. Please go and gather eggs."
    "Yes, Mama," said Little Grunt, and
off he went.

But eggs were hard to find. Little Grunt
looked and looked.
    "What am I going to do?" he asked himself.
"I can't find a single egg. I'll try one more place."

And it was a good thing that he did,
because there, in the one more place,
was the biggest egg Little Grunt had ever
seen. How would he ever get it home?
Eggs break *very* easily.

"I know," he said. He gathered some
thick pointy leaves and wove them into a
mat. He carefully rolled the egg on top of it.
Then he pulled and pulled and pulled the
egg all the way home.

"My goodness," said the Grunt Tribe. "Ooga, ooga! What an egg! That will feed us *and* the Ugga-Wuggas. And even the Grizzler Tribe. Maybe we should invite *them* to Sunday brunch, too."

"Ooga, ooga! Yummy! Yummy!" said the Grunts.

They put the egg near the fire and went to bed.

In the middle of the night, the egg began to make noise.

CLICK, CRACK. A big piece of shell fell to the floor.

CLICK, CRACK, CLUNK, PLOP. The egg broke in half.

And instead of the big egg sitting by the fire . . .

There was a baby dinosaur!

"Waaangh," cried the baby dinosaur.

And the Grunt Tribe all woke up.

"Ooga, ooga!" they said. "What's that?"

Chief Rockhead Grunt said, "All I know is
it can't stay . . ."

But before he could finish,
Little Grunt asked, "May I keep him?
Please? *Please?*"
   "Every boy needs a pet," said
Granny Grunt.

"Against my better judgment," mumbled
Chief Rockhead Grunt.

"I'm going to call him George," said Little Grunt.
Little Grunt and George became great pals.

But there was a problem. The cave stayed the
same size, but George didn't. He began to grow.

And **GROW.**

And **GROW.**

The cave got very crowded.

And there were other problems.
George wasn't housebroken.

George ate ALL the leaves off ALL the trees and ALL
the bushes ALL around the cave. And still he was hungry.

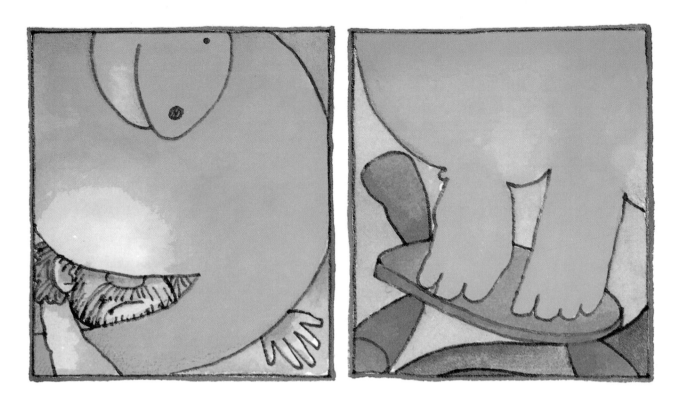

George liked to play—rough. George stepped on things.

And when he sneezed—well, it was a disaster.

"Ooga, ooga! Enough is enough!"
said the Grunts.

"I guess it wasn't a good idea to keep
him," said Granny Grunt. "How about a
nice *little* cockroach. They make nice pets."

"I'm in charge here,"
cried Chief Rockhead Grunt.
"And I say, *That giant lizard goes!*"
"Ooga, ooga! Yes! Yes!" said the Grunts.
"But you promised," said Little Grunt.

The next morning, Little Grunt took George back
to where he had found him.

"Good-bye, George," said Little Grunt.
"I'll sure miss you."

"Waaargh," said George.

Big tears rolled down their cheeks. Sadly, Little Grunt watched George walk slowly into the swamp.

"I'll never see him again," sobbed Little Grunt.

The days and months went by, and
Little Grunt still missed George.
He dreamed about him at night and
drew pictures of him by day.

"Little Grunt certainly misses that
dinosaur," said Mama Grunt.
"He'll get over it," said Papa Grunt.
"I still say a cockroach makes a nice pet,"
said Granny Grunt.

That night, the cave started to shake.
The floor began to pitch, and loud rumblings
filled the air.
"Earthquake!" cried the Grunts.

"No, it's not," said Granny Grunt. "Look! Volcano!"

Sure enough, steam, rocks, and black smoke shot
out of the top. Big rocks and huge boulders tumbled
and bounced around in front of the cave.

"We're trapped! We're trapped!" shouted
the Grunts. "What are we going to do?"
"Don't ask me!" said Chief Rockhead. "I resign."
"Now we have no leader," cried Ant Grunt.

"Now we're really in trouble!" shouted Papa Grunt, as lava poured out of the volcano in a wide, flaming river. It headed straight for the cave.

There was not enough time for the Grunts to escape.
All of a sudden, the Grunts heard a different noise.
"Waaargh! Wonk!"

"It's George!" cried Little Grunt. "He's come to save us."
"Ooga, ooga!" cried the Grunts.

They all ran to George and quickly filled up his long
neck, his long back, and his very long tail.

And before you could say Tyrannosaurus rex,

George carried them far away to safety.

"As your new leader," Papa Grunt said, "I say this is our new cave!"

"I like the kitchen," said Mama Grunt.

"When do we eat?" said Unca Grunt.

"I can't wait to start decorating," said Ant Grunt.

"I always say a change of scenery keeps you from getting old," said Granny Grunt.

"And George can live right next door," said Little Grunt.

"Where is George?" asked Mama Grunt.

"Ooga, ooga. Here, George," called the Grunts.

"Waaargh," answered George.

"Look!" said Little Grunt.
"Oh, no!" said the Grunts.

There was George, sitting on a pile of big eggs.
"I guess I'd better call George Georgina!"
said Little Grunt.

And they all lived happily ever after.